KEPT *by the* BEAST

HALLIE BENNETT

BOOKS BY THIS AUTHOR

CHAPTER ONE

POPPY

Cool, fall air sifts through my hair after rolling the car window down for the drive home. Earlier, I decided to take a break from being a hermit in my apartment and drove thirty minutes to the cute mountain town of High Ridge for some shopping. Rife with unique shops and picturesque views, the small town evokes Hallmark-esque vibes, and more than once, I considered how nice it'd be to live here.

City life isn't terrible—full of fun events and opportunities to meet people. Which is why I moved to Everton in the first place, except I never followed through with actually partaking in those events. Striking up conversations with strangers is extremely difficult for me, and the few friends I have aren't very social either—uninterested in attending anything.

If I'm not taking advantage of city living, I might as well enjoy beautiful views in a smaller town.

Images of my idyllic life in High Ridge float through my mind until a bang shakes the car, scaring me to death, while I quickly pull over to the side of the road as the vehicle's speed declines. Dense forest surrounds me, and the pretty seasonal colors I admired on my way here no longer hold their appeal. Instead, they signal my unfortunate luck of being stranded in the middle of nowhere.

I decided against taking the major highway because I wanted to meander through country roads, but now I'm regretting that decision. Shifting to park, quiet settles over me as a wave of anxiety rushes forward. What do I do now?

Cars have never been my thing, and I've been blessed with a trouble-free record. Until now. Regret for never purchasing a Triple A membership assaults me.

Damn my procrastination.

Stupid.

Squeezing the steering wheel tightly, I consider my options which, admittedly, are slim. Hermits aren't known for their large circles of friends, right? Not for the first time, I lament my lack of social skills.

Stop having a pity party and think. Try calling Tory.

Out of a short list of friends, she's the one I'm closest to. Scrolling to her contact information, the phone rings a few times before she answers with a breezy greeting. Suddenly, my throat closes in embarrassment and an intense aversion to asking for help. It feels like I'm intruding on her life with a problem I should have been able to prevent—paying for Triple A—or figure out on my own.

"Hello?"

Exhaling harshly, I choke the words out, attempting a cheerful tone. "Hey! Sorry to bother you, but my car just died on the side of the road back from High Ridge. Is there any way you could come and possibly jump my car?"

"That sucks! You don't have roadside assistance? My parents pay for mine, and it's been a lifesaver. Especially with the car I have now. I don't think it'll be a good idea to try to jump yours.

It could fry mine or yours or both. Maybe you can try someone else?"

Jumbled emotions flutter in my stomach. Envy that she has parents who offer to pay for such a car service. Humiliation at being turned down, knowing she was my best bet for help. And worry about what to do next.

But I don't let Tory know anything's wrong. Forcing a laugh, I brush it off. "No worries; I'll figure something out. Thanks, though!"

Hanging up, desperation and panic ratchet higher as the only other people I feel a modicum of comfort requesting help from can't come to my aid. Jessica's out of town and Nadine doesn't have jumper cables. A thought of suggesting she buy cables, so I can reimburse her later enters my head, but I dismiss it. She'd already be doing me a favor driving out here; I can't expect her to stop by the store, too.

Tears overflow down my cheeks, I hate how alone and pathetic I am.

Who doesn't have at least one person they can call when they need help? How could I be so dumb and not have a contingency plan for this sort of thing?

Resting my head on the back of the seat, orange sunlight blinds me as the sun starts to set. *Better hurry and call an auto shop before they close.* It's Friday and nearing five pm; I can't sit here frozen—no matter how helpless I feel.

Thankfully, my phone has service as I search auto body shops. *At least that's one good thing.* But before I can contact a shop, the phone vibrates and a blue screen appears.

Oh, no.

This happens every once in a while when it decides to randomly restart but gets stuck on one screen. There's no way for me to get around it. I have to wait for it to die because charging the phone from zero usually brings it back to life. Too bad I've been charging it in my car all day in case of an emergency. Joke's on me because here I am in a legitimate crisis without a working phone.

Groaning in anguish, a headache pounds behind my eyes from the tears and stress overloading my body. All I wanted was a relaxing day out—something I never do because I talk myself out of going places if I'll be alone. Instead, circumstances remind me how lonely, foolish, and pathetic I am.

Is walking my only option? I don't remember seeing much civilization behind me, but what else is there? Check under the hood?

I don't know much about cars, but maybe it'll be something obvious like a cap popped off or low coolant. Filling the bottle up with the blue liquid isn't beyond my limited skills. It's literally the only thing I can do besides airing up my tires when the lights show low tire pressure.

Glancing around the driver's seat, I try to remember how to even pop the hood when a button with a car and opened hood catches my eye. The button causes a loud click as the top jumps up. Hustling towards the front of the vehicle, my hand skims underneath the warm metal until my fingers meet the latch that lets me raise the hood above my head. I prop it up and scan the collection of black parts, praying a problem jumps out at me.

No such luck.

Head hanging in dejection, an engine rumbles ahead when a dark blue truck slowly approaches to park behind the car. My heart rate skyrockets as a large man hops down from the truck cab, and past murder documentaries I've binged rear their ugly heads.

"You need some help?" The stranger's gruff voice jerks me to attention, a trembling hand covering my heart as if to slow its chaotic beating. A thick beard covers the lower part of his face while auburn waves shaggily fall to brush his shoulders.

Do I say yes? No? I'm stranded, and he's the first person to appear since my car trouble started. How likely is it that he's a serial killer versus a good Samaritan?

"Uh, yes, thank you. I'm not sure what's wrong." He edges around the grey fender, and I hurry out of his way, keeping a short distance between us. Up close, his hulking form is even more obvious and intimidating.

Tall with broad shoulders, his barrel chest tapers down to thighs thick as tree trunks. For once in my life, I actually feel petite compared to him, and at a size twenty in jeans, I'm not a small woman.

"Let's take a look. I'm Asa, by the way."

"Poppy."

He tinkers with a couple of caps and lines before clucking his tongue and stepping back. "Nothing stands out as obviously wrong, though I'm no expert. Let me try to give you a jump; we'll see if it starts. Unfortunately, all the local car shops are probably closed by now. Is there someone you can call to pick you up?"

No, because I'm pathetic.

Tears threaten to spill over again, and I quickly swipe at them, turning to the side in the hope that he doesn't see them.

Words stutter from my throat. "I'll probably try getting an Uber."

If I ever get my phone to work.

"We don't have a lot of Ubers around here... Hey, are you okay?" A gentle hand cups my shoulder, guiding me to face him, but I keep my face averted until another hand lifts my chin. Embarrassment heats my cheeks as he witnesses my breakdown.

"I'm fine." An annoying warble clings to my voice, betraying the lie. "What if it starts with the jump? It should be okay to drive to Everton, right? It's not that far of a trip."

"I wouldn't risk it; you're stranded here because something's wrong. It wouldn't be safe for you if it happens again on a busy highway." His head gives a negative shake as my shoulders sag. Concern over stranger danger becomes consumed by worry. What am I going to do?

"I'm sure it'll be fine. Maybe this incident was a fluke. A jump would be much appreciated, then I'll be on my way." Maybe I'll get lucky and make it home without any more trouble. Or at least be close enough that Tory might rescue me from the side of a different road. At this point, screw the car. I'd accept a ride home where I can hide in my bed, avoiding responsibility until tomorrow.

Asa's jaw clenches in disapproval at my decision, but it's not like he has much choice. Unless he plans on leaving me here.

"Okay, here's what we're going to do. We'll jump your car and hope it starts, then I'll follow you home to ensure you arrive safely."

"You can't do that! That'll be an hour out of your way." *Way too much to ask of a good Samaritan.* "Trust me, I'll be fine, and if not, maybe a state trooper will stop to help next time. Either way, it's not your problem to solve, though I appreciate the offer." My stomach's already tangled in knots; I don't need to heap on more stress and embarrassment by letting this man go so far out of his way to help.

"No deal. You want the jump; you let me make sure you get home safely."

"And if I don't agree, you'll leave me stranded here? How's that much better?"

"If you don't agree, I'm hauling you home with me. Your choice."

My previous fear roars to the forefront, but this time it drags along a curious companion: excitement. Arousal is just heightened senses, right? From fear or attraction, my body suddenly comes to life in an unexpected way.

Are you serious right now?

Despite him being a stranger, a part of me would love nothing more than to trust he's a good man and put myself in his hands—to let him takeover. But I can't allow myself the fantasy. It's not right or safe.

And really, it's a vague statement. *Haul you home with me.* He could mean until I find someone to pick me up. Or to stash me in his basement. Or to stretch me out on his bed for a good, long fucking.

The possibilities are endless.

And this mountain air and crisis have officially demolished any common sense you have.

CHAPTER TWO

ASA

Insanity must be rotting my brain...*or lust.*

What other explanation can there be for saying such an idiotic thing? The woman hardly knows me, and I threaten to take her home. Practically fucking kidnapping her. You'd think my previous encounters with women—the ones where they warily eye my size and retreat—would make me smarter. But I guess not.

Because this curvy little bombshell slipped past any reason and has gone straight to the caveman portion of my brain. The part that thinks it's okay to throw her over my shoulder before tying her to my bed. Apparently, the Beast—the name some townspeople whisper behind my back—is tired of being alone, wants a mate, and has chosen Poppy.

Poppy—a fragile flower that my fucking bear paws could crush.

Before I can apologize for the aggressive dictate, she answers, "We'll do it your way." I freeze. She wants to go home with me? My dick twitches in eagerness, rising to the occasion. "You can follow behind me in case anything happens on the drive."

Right, you fucking idiot. She wants to go home, not to bed with your ugly mug.

"Sounds good, let me get my jumper cables," I mumble and head back to my truck, grabbing the tools before returning. She's dried her cheeks, though remnants of her crying remain. The sight of her pain is like a vise around my heart—crushing it under the pressure—and I want to cuddle her sweet curves close to protect her from any more harm.

Five minutes later, the car refuses to start which means our earlier argument is moot. Part of it, anyway, because I still want to steal Poppy back to my cabin.

Her forehead rests on the steering wheel, defeat clear in the line of her drooping shoulders. Giving her a moment of privacy, I step away to call my friend and business partner, Micah.

"Hey, man, what's up?"

"Are you busy? There's a woman stranded on the side of 85 and could use a tow."

"And you've elected yourself as her knight in shining armor? Doesn't sound like you." Micah laughs, but he's not wrong. Since women avoid me, I do the same. Enough of their fearful or snide remarks have reached my ears in passing that I don't need to seek it out by approaching them.

Growing up, I always felt set apart. My family was dirt poor, living in a ramshackle trailer on the side of the mountain. When I was old enough, I helped when I could by pitching in at the local lumberyard with my dad, and it wasn't long before the added bulk from hard labor combined with my height to form the town's Beast.

"Fuck off," I say with little heat. "Can you help or not?"

"Yeah, just text me the location." Thanking him, I end the call and see how Poppy's doing. Dusk has fallen, and we'll be sitting ducks out here the later it becomes. This road doesn't get a lot of traffic which means drivers think it's okay to speed through the winding curves. Every year multiple accidents occur, and I don't want us to be around when complete darkness hits.

"So, my friend's bringing his truck to tow your car, since we can't leave it here." Recklessness pervades my thoughts again as I continue, "You can stay the night with me. In the morning, we can talk to the town mechanic about your car."

The gentlemanly thing to do would be to offer to drive her all the way home, which I'll do if she insists, but if she doesn't... Well, I'm not above having her under my roof, preferably under *me* as I drive my cock into her wet pussy.

Fuck.

This is what celibacy gets me: lusting after a woman I barely know but can't resist craving.

"Okay." The lone word is dull with acceptance; obviously, she's over the whole ordeal. And shame creeps in at my dirty thoughts. Poppy doesn't need me panting over her, eager to fuck. She needs a comforting shoulder and a helping hand. That's it.

"You said you live in Everton. What brings you to High Ridge?" I ask, trying to get her mind off the situation while we wait for help to arrive.

"I like your downtown Main Street; it's really cute. So, I thought it'd be a nice break from the city to explore the local shops."

"Find anything good?"

"Not worth the trouble it's caused me," she mutters under her breath. "Some. A lot of places had fun fall decorations that I grabbed."

"That's good." I search for something else to add when Micah finally pulls in front of Poppy's car. *Thank god.* I don't know much about girly shit like home decor. My knowledge taps out around basic construction which is why I don't handle that side of business. Micah and his brother, Rhett, co-own a joint lumber and construction company with me, and I stick to what I know: raw wood.

Micah hops out of the cab and waves before heading towards the rear and messing with jangling chains. "We better hurry; we don't have much light."

Nodding, I help him hook her car to the tow as Poppy watches from the side of the road after grabbing the essentials from the vehicle. Arms cross her chest as she rubs gloved hands over the sleeves in an effort to stay warm as the temperature drops.

"Baby, why don't you wait in my truck where there's heat. We won't be much longer."

"Are you sure? We're strangers; I could be a secret car thief."

Micah and I laugh at the ridiculous notion. She'd be the cutest car thief I've ever seen. "I'll risk it. Here, take these." I toss her the keys from my pocket and watch as she clambers inside the raised truck, the loud hum of the engine revving to life.

"*Baby*, huh? The women of High Ridge will be heartbroken at the sight of their Beast in love." He teases as we finish securing the vehicle.

"I'm not in love," I scoff, slapping cold hands against my thighs to wipe the dirt from the chains away. *But hardcore lust coated in a heavy layer of possessiveness? Hell yes.*

"Not yet..." Micah tips his head knowingly. "I can drop this off at the mechanic's by myself while you see to your girl."

"Thanks, I owe you one." Waving good-bye, I jog back to the truck and climb into the driver's seat, heat wafting over my freezing nose and cheeks. Country music plays softly in the background as Poppy plays with her phone, the blue screen looking ominous even from here.

"How are you doing? I know this isn't ideal, but I promise you're safe with me. And we'll figure everything out tomorrow."

"I hope so. I hate infringing on your time like this; I'm so sorry."

"You're not infringing on anything, and you definitely don't need to apologize. I stepped in and offered to help because I wanted to." When I'd spotted her lone car on the shoulder of the road earlier, it'd been tempting to pass it by. My history with the townspeople doesn't incline me to come to their aid, but I figured I might be one of the few cars to frequent this section of the interstate and reluctantly stopped.

Best decision you've made in a while.

The rest of the drive stays quiet as I navigate the sharp turns that lead to my cabin. Once inside the austere interior, we shed our coats and gloves before I lead her on a short tour that ends in the master bedroom. "Here's your room. The master bath's through there. Feel free to use whatever you want or borrow any clothes."

"The master? I don't want to take your room. Why don't I sleep on the couch—"

"Not an option. You'll have this room, and I'll take the spare. No arguments." I can't explain the rationale to her. All I know is if I can't share a bed with her tonight, at least her scent will be all over my pillows and sheets, and I'll take whatever I can get. Keeping a part of her once she leaves.

If she leaves... My mind revisits the idea of chaining her to my bed like a caveman before I shake it away.

Confusion darkens her expression as a mulish line forms on her mouth, but she stays silent. "Alright... thank you, again. If it's okay, I think I just want to go to sleep despite the early hour..." Her growling stomach interrupts, and a scarlet flush blooms on her cheeks.

"Why don't I whip up something to eat, then you can turn in for the night?"

Poppy agrees, and the rest of the night flies by between stunted conversations and dinner. I try not to let it affect me, but for the first time, I regret my lack of experience with women. Small talk is already a struggle but trying to communicate with a woman I'm interested in? Even more fucking difficult.

Sighing, I shelf the fantasy of keeping her.

Who'd want to stay with the Beast?

CHAPTER THREE

POPPY

A fitful night of sleep follows last night's debacle, and I dread what will come today. The only good news is that my phone seems to be working again after Asa let me borrow his charger, and there's one message from Tory asking what happened with the car. After responding, I toss the phone aside and stare at the ceiling—more tears threatening to spill over.

Geez, will you get over yourself?

Crying seems to be the only thing I can do lately, but I can't help it. Only one person cared enough to check on me. *One.* I could literally disappear, and no one would wonder where I've gone. Hell, I'm currently lying in a stranger's bed with no one the wiser. Ironically, the knowledge that I'm residing in a man's home isn't my top worry. Asa seems like a decent guy, verging on a saint with as much as he's helping me.

No, I'm more concerned with my lack of a social life and what to do about my car as my gaze wanders over the ceiling above.

Wooden beams span the room, adding to the rustic feel of the cabin and creating a cozy warmth that the large bed enhances with its fluffy pillows and heavy blankets. If only that comforting embrace had alleviated my stress and anxiety during the night or even the pity I'm feeling for myself currently.

Sighing in resignation, I throw off the covers and prepare to face the day. Asa mentioned last night visiting the mechanic's garage once they opened at ten this morning. The clock on my phone reads eight-thirty, so there's still some time to kill.

Wandering around the room, it reflects the same bare-bones layout as downstairs. Nothing adorns the walls, and it's clear Asa believes in function only. There isn't a piece in the cabin that doesn't serve a useful purpose—unlike my apartment in Everton.

Hoards of knick knacks populate every nook and cranny of my home. Honestly, I probably shouldn't have bought the seasonal decorations yesterday because my place doesn't have any more free space. But it's hard to walk away from cute foxes and owls especially when shopping gives me a nice boost of endorphins.

Something in short supply lately.

Ambling across the hardwood floor, a curious noise draws me to the window. My breathing stutters to a halt at the sight before me. Asa stands shirtless, chopping short blocks of wood like a lumberjack.

A hot as hell giant of a lumberjack.

Sweat drips down his chest despite the cool temperature, glistening in the mat of dark curls that trail down to the button of his jeans. He lifts the axe above his head and brings it down again with a loud thwack causing me to jump at the sound. Muscles flex in his shoulders and arms as he removes the split halves of wood and adds another block.

Stop watching. Don't be weird.

But it's difficult to look away. I've never seen a man like him—like this—up close and personal. Truthfully, I thought they only lived in the fantasies of my dreams or books and movies. Yet, the dream had come to life in this flesh and blood man who rescued me from an uncertain fate last night.

If I were a different kind of woman, I'd figure out how to use this to my advantage, but that just feels icky considering his good nature so far. He didn't sign up to get manipulated or used by me—a needy virgin who's too plump for her own good. Best to long for things I can have from afar, safely ensconced in this room.

Without warning, he glances towards me, and I pivot away from the glass pane, back banging into the wall. *Please don't let him see me.* All I need is for Asa to know I was spying on him. Long minutes pass before my heart rate returns to normal, and I chance another peek outside.

He's no longer there which explains the abrupt silence. My eyes close in relief as I slide down the wall like a glob of jelly. Footsteps stomp down the hall before a door closes, and pipes rattle in the walls as a shower starts.

Don't even go there, I warn before my mind conjures images of a naked Asa. *Think about your dead car. About your adult responsibilities.* Unfortunately, those incite anxiety instead of the pleasant rush of hormones Asa sets off.

I wait until the shower turns off and Asa goes back downstairs before deciding it's time to follow him. It's closer to the time we need to leave, so hopefully, there won't be a lot of awkward moments until then. Especially now that I've seen him bare-chested and imagined what the rest would look like without all the denim and flannel.

If I had a problem with being tongue-tied prior to the lumberjack scene, I'm really screwed now. But hiding in his room isn't exactly the smartest move either. Better to face him and get this day over with.

I quickly pull on the same jeans from yesterday but keep the cozy button-down of Asa's that I'm wearing—tying the overly long ends into a knot that rests at my hips. The need for such a thing makes me smile. I might've found the one man whose clothing actually dwarfs me, and the unfamiliar sensation lets me feel petite for once in my life.

Heading down the stairs, I find Asa stacking a couple of split logs beside the fireplace. "Good morning." My hand lifts in a short wave of greeting, gauging his reaction to my arrival. *Did he see me watching him earlier?*

"Morning. How'd you sleep?"

"As well as expected." His demeanor remains relaxed, and relief calms some of the worry in my gut.

"That good, huh?" A commiserating grin softens his rough-hewn features, and the effect it has on my heart sends me reeling. Though not classically attractive, Asa exudes a raw aura of masculinity that my body can't help responding to—blood racing, nerves tingling, preparing to receive him like I'm in heat.

Is my period starting soon?

I inwardly chuckle at the thought. Thinking of sex isn't out of the ordinary but these types of sensations usually increase in frequency around that time of the month. *Or it could just be the man...* Either way, my body needs to chill and let my brain focus on what matters: my car troubles.

"If you're ready to go, I figured we could grab breakfast at the diner next door to the garage. By the time we're done eating, it should be open for us to talk to the mechanic on duty." Asa straightens to his full height and slaps the dust from his hands, eyes travelling over my body before meeting my gaze.

Flushing at the inspection, I manage a jerky nod. "Sounds good to me."

The sooner my car's fixed, the better, because the longer I'm here, the greater the chance I embarrass myself with the chaos of hormones flooding my system in his presence. And that would be truly mortifying.

An active man like him? Not interested in chubby and shy, I'm sure.

CHAPTER FOUR

ASA

Poppy looks like a fucking pinup for a special flannel edition of Playboy—one specifically made for me. And I'm ready to turn to the centerfold.

The shirt she's wearing is mine, and it's knotted at her waist, showcasing an exaggerated hourglass shape I want to lick until my name's a plea in her throat. Not the first time today I've envisioned that particular fantasy either. An image of her from this morning is burned in my memory. Outlined by glowing light and framed perfectly in the window, Poppy had been a vision—still clothed in my shirt but her legs exposed under the hem.

It had taken all of my strength and resolve to walk past her bedroom door instead of breaking it down to fall on her like a hungry wolf. Instead, I made do with jerking off in the shower which was a sad substitute for the warm woman in my bed.

Stealing another peek at Poppy across the truck console, my knuckles turn white as I clutch the steering wheel in an effort to not reach over and hold her hand. The innocent gesture is a marked change from my filthier thoughts but no less appealing.

"So, when you're not visiting High Ridge, what do you do? I know Everton's known for its tech companies. Is that something you're interested in?" I ask, thirsty for more information about her life. It occurs to me that she could have a boyfriend back home, but if she did, he's clearly not worth a damn after leaving her so helpless and unprotected.

Doesn't matter now. She's mine. Finders keepers and all that shit.

"Not really. I'm a freelance editor for authors, so at least I won't be required to show up at an office Monday morning if this ordeal drags on that long." Her body stiffens as she immediately apologizes. "Sorry, I didn't mean for that to sound so harsh. You've been great; I just hate ruining your weekend."

"Trust me, you haven't ruined anything." *Quite the opposite.* She's upended my world in the best possible way. Inexplicably and with no effort. There isn't a logical explanation for the way I feel about Poppy—just a primal knowledge she belongs to me. All I need to do is help her realize that truth.

Preferably before she has a means to escape me.

"What about you? High Ridge is pretty small. Do you commute somewhere?"

"Not often. I'm part owner in Olson-Keller Lumber & Construction. Our lumberyard is about fifteen minutes from town, and most of my responsibilities lie there." The hard, physical labor comforts me—a holdover from my youth spent doing similar work with my dad.

"That explains so much."

"It does?"

Poppy stammers out an explanation as I park at the diner. "Oh... Um... It just makes sense that a lumber company would be successful in a small mountain community, that's all. And the need for materials or crews to build never really fades either."

"Neither does a supply of authors needing editors, I suppose. Plus, you're free to work wherever." *Like here with me when we're not busy fucking.*

"That's one of the reasons I moved to Everton. I thought it'd be good for me to live somewhere with more social opportunities to make friends, since my work life is so flexible. It's nice being free to work when and where I want, except it usually means staying home ninety-nine percent of the time." A dejected note creeps into her voice, and sympathy for her plight crowds my chest. Hearing her unhappiness strengthens my determination to keep her.

I'll care for Poppy. Ensure her satisfaction. I may not have any experience keeping a woman, but I'll learn damn fast to assure her needs are met.

"No boyfriend to take you out for date nights?" I probe, body suspended in apprehension.

A self-deprecating laugh bursts from her. "Definitely not. I barely have any friends to hang out with... Actually, forget I said that. I'm not sure why I'm sharing so much; it's not your problem." She struggles unbuckling the seatbelt, fidgeting in her seat, and I stop resisting my instincts.

Reaching across the console, my hand engulfs hers in a comforting squeeze. "Don't worry about it. I like the insight into your life and appreciate you entrusting me with such vulnerability." Doubt darkens her expression; it'll take more than words to convince Poppy. "The same can be said for me. Micah and Rhett are the only people I rely on, and our bond formed after being branded as the town's dark sheep."

"How does an entire town decide that?"

"When you don't fit their mold, it's fairly easy. So, I understand feeling left out or lonely." Something I'd never admitted out loud—the depth of the emotion previously unexplored. While I ignored most of the locals' opinions of me, it left a mark being an outcast.

"I'm sorry that's been your experience here. It sucks, doesn't it?" Her hand turns over, fingers lacing with mine. "What a pair we make."

A mated pair.

I lift our entwined hands to rub the back of hers along my cheek before reluctantly letting go, so we can head inside the diner. Fancy's is one of the few places I frequent in town because the old-timers and regulars don't give a shit about town politics and mind their own business. If a hankering for social interaction arises—a rare occasion—visiting the diner soothes the need even if I'm sitting alone in a booth. Just the act of being around people is enough.

Leading Poppy to my usual spot, she slides over the cracked plastic seat while I settle across from her. Sticky menus lay in front of us, and it's not long before our orders are placed and delivered. We stick to lighter topics after the conversation earlier, content with learning about the other in a less serious way.

Bells ring as the diner door opens to reveal Mindy and her posse. *What the fuck are they doing here?* Part of the country club set, this place seems below their snobby standards. My jaw clenches when Mindy notices me, her narrowed eyes travelling over my tense shoulders before landing on Poppy. Ever since high school, she's led the charge of naming me *Beast* and encouraging others to do the same.

I recognize the calculating gleam in her eyes and brace for an attack. Eventually Poppy would encounter my moniker, but I wish she would've had a little more time getting to know me beforehand.

"Ladies, be careful. The Beast left his lair." The trio of women titter in amusement as they walk past our table. "Should we warn his prey to run while she can?"

A low growl vibrates in the back of my throat at the threat.

"Is she talking about you?" Poppy asks in disbelief, following the path of the women as they find a table near the back.

"Yeah, it's their stupid pet name for me."

"But why?"

I sweep a hand down my chest—encompassing my large form—hating having to explain to her. I don't want her to see a beast, but it's inevitable. "Isn't it obvious? I'm an ugly fucking giant. Have been for years. Women either run in fear or revulsion. I'm just thankful you haven't."

Yet.

She releases a shaky breath, and a flush spreads from her neck to her cheeks. "You're not ugly. And you don't deserve that kind of treatment." Her words vibrate in anger, and the fierce reaction surprises me. Fury seems like a foreign emotion for Poppy with how concerned she's been about not causing me trouble this weekend. But I guess everyone has their limit, and we might've reached hers.

"Just ignore them; I usually do."

"I don't want to. They can't come in here and insult you for fun. It's like a scene from Mean Girls." She bites her lip in contemplation before a steely look glimmers in her eyes. "Two questions: Do you want to really give them something to talk about? And do you trust me?"

"Unequivocally yes, but I'm not sure what you—"

Poppy scrambles out of her seat and rounds the table before plopping down beside me, practically in my lap. Wrapping a hand around my neck, she pulls me down until her lips press hard against mine. I immediately open to the advance—partly in shock but mostly in greedy acceptance—and her tongue pushes forward, tasting of maple syrup from her waffles.

Fucking delicious.

Any thoughts of Mindy and her gang fly out the window as all of my senses focus on Poppy. Sucking the sweetness from her tongue. Reveling in the heat of her body. The curve of a breast bumps my arm, and I long to slip between the buttons of her shirt to cup the heavy weight in my palm. But we're in public.

Would a beast care when his mate's so close?

No, he fucking wouldn't.

Resolve disappearing, my fingertips graze a button before Poppy retreats—returned as quickly to her seat as she left it. And a rumble of displeasure rolls around my chest.

Come back.

CHAPTER FIVE

POPPY

A pleasant buzz tingles along my nerve endings as I sink back into my seat after kissing Asa. My first kiss, and I decided to initiate it in front of an audience. *What is happening to me?*

First, I share the embarrassing fact of having hardly any friends, then I kiss the man in public? It's like High Ridge has become a portal to a new me—a less guarded, more daring Poppy. Which is a strange revelation.

Shocked stares come from the women in the back, and satisfaction infuses my blood. I hate conflict, preferring to lay low and go with the flow, but bullies are the exception. And those women? Major bullies.

When I heard what they called Asa, I saw red—something I'm not used to—and my only thought was to make him feel better. *Which, of course, meant kissing the man.* My logic might have been off, but I don't regret the action. The savory flavor of his mouth lingers in mine, and Asa certainly didn't seem to mind the aggressive move.

"Hopefully, that was okay." I gulp the last of my glass of water, hoping to cool my temper and arousal.

"Hell, yes. Feel free to jump me again whenever you please."

"I'll keep that in mind." We both laugh, and the mutual attraction is palpable between us—a feeling that's unfamiliar.

For some reason, Asa seems to like me despite my lack of social skills and a body that's seen the inside of a kitchen more than the gym. Though maybe I shouldn't be so surprised. His admission of feeling lonely and left out echo my own as if we're two kindred spirits.

"We're about done here. Fred's shop should be open by now if you're ready to hear the verdict on your car." Nodding, remembering the true reason I'm here, I start to pull out my wallet when Asa extracts his with a shake of his head and throws down payment for breakfast.

Thanking him with a smile, we walk next door to the garage where an older man stands behind a counter. "Morning, folks. How can I help you?"

"The grey Camry out there belongs to Poppy and needs to be looked at as soon as possible. It stalled out on Route 85 yesterday." I appreciate Asa stepping in to answer the man's question—taking the lead. Even if it's unfair or distinctly anti-feministic, the apprehension in my body melts away. I really didn't want to explain things myself when I don't know what the hell I'm talking about.

"Ah, I noticed it outside. It'll be a few hours before I can take a look, then it probably won't be until Monday before it's fixed. There's a line of cars ahead of you, and the shop's open short hours today and closed tomorrow." The man shrugs apologetically, but I understand. Small towns operate differently than larger cities, moving at a slower pace. "If you have the keys, I'll take those and your number to call with the issues and cost to repair."

Handing the keys over, I write down my phone number with Asa adding his below it, and ten minutes later we're back at his truck—wondering what to do next.

"I know you explored Main Street yesterday, so unless there was something you missed or want to revisit, I could show you the lumberyard." Piles of wood don't sound particularly appealing but spending time alone with Asa? I'll take it.

"Sure, let's go."

He opens the truck door and helps me step into the high cab, large hands spanning my waist. I swear his grip tightens for a moment before loosening, and butterflies knock around my belly—staying the entire drive out to the lumberyard.

Pallets of logs and boards line one side of the vast complex while heavy machinery is neatly parked in rows along a large garage. Tires crunch over coarse gravel before Asa parks in front of a medium-sized building at the center of it all.

"Here we are—the official home of Olson-Keller Lumber & Construction. This used to be acres of forest before we built everything." Exiting the vehicle, we stroll towards an entryway as I study the tamed landscape.

"This might sound rude, but do you guys do anything to offset cutting down all these trees?"

"We try to be eco-conscious and plant two trees for every one we cut. To be honest, I never really thought about those things until becoming an owner in the company, and we received tons of notices from local environmental groups. But it's become a priority for us, since we've been educated." He holds the door open before following me inside a combined space of waiting chairs and desks.

I appreciate his willingness to learn and adapt especially when it's not a skill everyone has. It endeared him to me that much more. *As if you needed one more reason to like him.*

"It's awesome you guys have taken the information and incorporated it into actual change for your company. Very impressive." Walking around the area, my eyes jump from desk to desk before asking, "Which one's yours?"

He points to a desk in front of a window, devoid of anything except for a closed laptop. "I don't spend a lot of time here which is why it's so bare."

"Not even a picture, though you do have a pretty view." Black Mountain stands tall and majestic awash in fall colors—orange, red, and yellow leaves turned for the season.

"Agreed." Asa's hot breath skims over my neck, his body much nearer than before. His hand tentatively touches my hip as if waiting for me to rebuff the move, but I stay still and say nothing. The warm weight roves forward until his palm cups my breast, fingertips toying with the buttons of the shirt over my open coat.

"This is what I wanted to do at the diner, but you left too soon." The disgruntled words spark a moment of amusement—his tone like a boy who'd lost his favorite toy—until he nimbly undoes the buttons and slips a hand under the flannel.

"If you'd done this at the diner, I'm pretty sure we would've been banned for life." He tweaks a nipple through the thin fabric of my sports bra, and I lament the absence of something sexier. But it's not like I planned on getting stranded and subsequently rescued by a lumberjack wanting to touch me.

"Their loss." Asa nips my earlobe, the sudden pain momentarily distracts me from his other hand working its way beneath the waist of my jeans and panties. How far is he going to take this?

How far am I willing to let him take this?

And the answer comes immediately: *All the way.*

Our time together in High Ridge is limited. My car will be fixed soon, and I'll be headed home. And who knows how long this brave Poppy will stick around? Best to experience everything I can before she disappears and fear takes her place.

Tilting my head to the side to give him more access, I sink deeper into his body, his height forming the perfect curve to mine. My hands roam backward and firm muscle greets me. I can't resist tugging his hips closer to rub my ass against the hard erection nestled in the crease of my jeans. It's a brazen move—uncharacteristic of me—but he clearly approves with a squeeze of my breast and rumbled growl of pleasure.

"You're begging to be fucked, baby." Asa's fingers spear through my slick folds to reach their prize, and a keening gasp escapes at the contact. Rough fingertips. Sensitive nerves. The combination ignites a spark like nothing I've encountered before.

My own touch doesn't come close.

Needing him to feel the same, I unbutton his jeans to wrap a trembling hand around him—the first cock I've held. "Am I? I can't help it.'

"I know... You need me—my hard dick tunneling deep into this wet pussy—don't you? But you're going to have to settle for this until we get home." He circles my clit before dipping lower, and my grip on him tightens involuntarily as I try to ride his fingers at the explicit imagery. To think one little kiss brought us to this flashpoint.

Perhaps I should thank Mindy and her minions...

"As long as you're with me." I don't want to be the only one to enjoy this short interlude; I want to please him, too. There's an awkward angle between us, so I turn around to face him, his hands quickly recapturing their former bounties.

"Always."

CHAPTER SIX

ASA

I'm struggling to keep it together with her hand sliding up and down my erection, squeezing firmly. Her touch is so different from my own—lighter, softer—yet somehow more intense because it's Poppy's hand, not mine.

"Don't stop, baby." *Please, don't ever stop.*

She strokes faster in an effort to comply, arching into me. And my attention returns to my original goal—playing with her tits. They're hidden behind a plain black sports bra, though hard buds clearly poke at the fabric. Tugging the elastic top down, it settles beneath her breasts, pushing them higher, puffy nipples begging for my mouth.

Hungry for a taste, I lick along a plump curve before reaching its pink tip and sucking it deep. I've never done this before. Never tasted a woman's delicate flesh. Never felt a woman's slick cream coat my fingers.

But experiencing this with Poppy? A growl of pleasure resounds in my chest. I want to satisfy her and pray I can figure out what she needs by paying attention to her reactions.

Rubbing circles around her clit, she gasps at the move, her hand choking me firmly in response. I inhale a deep breath; I don't want to come before she does. Besides being humiliating, that's not how I want to treat my woman.

Fingers travelling back down, I ease them into her clasping sheath and imagine my cock in the vise-like hold. *It'll come. Just be patient.*

Thrusting in and out, I search for the sensitive patch inside, recognizing it when she jerks. I increase pressure on the spot as my palm slaps against her clit. The speed of our motions escalate, each anticipating the other's impending climax.

"Come, little flower. My sweet Poppy. Come for me..." The whispered demand grazes her ear as her breath hitches, and I know she's close.

"Hello? Asa? I saw your truck outside and—" I immediately snatch my hands back and block Poppy from Rhett's view while struggling to stuff my cock into my jeans before turning to face him.

What great fucking timing.

"Sorry, I didn't mean to interrupt anything," Rhett apologizes, though the stern look in his eyes says he's feeling anything but remorseful. If I walked in on him or Micah messing around with a woman in the office, my face might have that same pissed-off expression, but I can't regret touching my woman.

"It's cool. We were just leaving."

Poppy shuffles forward, hurrying past Rhett with an awkward wave, and I follow at a more sedate pace.

"This is the kind of shit I'd expect from Micah, not you. Who is that woman?"

"Her name's Poppy, and get used to seeing her because she's mine." Might as well lay my cards on the table.

"Yours?" Disbelief drips from his voice as he runs an agitated hand through his short hair. Rhett may be as thick as I am, but he's the slightly shorter, cleaner cut version of me? the non-Beast of High Ridge. We've been best friends forever while Micah, his younger brother, tagged along. "How'd you manage to find her in this town?"

"She was stranded on the side of the road. Outside of town." I grin at the distinction, and Rhett chuckles with a shake of his head. "Now, if you'll excuse me, I've got some unfinished business to attend to."

Like claiming my mate with a long bout of fucking.

Poppy's waiting by the side of the truck, her hands tucked into her coat. "Is he one of your partners?"

"Yeah, he's Micah's older brother, Rhett." Unlocking the truck, I help her inside the lifted cab and hurry to the driver's side. "You'll get to know him later."

Unexpectedly, a giggle fills the space between us as she tries to cover a laugh. "I feel like we're teenagers who just got caught doing something we shouldn't have. Was he very angry?"

"Nah, we're good. And while I can't speak from experience, I suppose you're right about the teenagers comparison. But at least we're adults now. Free to do whatever the fuck we please. Like go home and continue, if that's what you want." A niggle of doubt works its way into my mind that Poppy might come to her senses. That she might realize allowing the Beast's lowly touch isn't what she wants.

"It is."

Two words, but they rock my foundation down to the depths of my soul.

"How long will it take us to get home?"

Home. I like the sound of her referring to my cabin as our home. Especially since it's at the top of my list of things to do: first, fuck her, then keep her beside me always.

"Twenty minutes or so."

"Hmm... I don't think I can wait that long..." Poppy's hand drifts over her coat and still partially unbuttoned shirt until it slides under her jeans, and my breath stammers in my lungs. What the fuck is she doing?

The wet sound of her fingers slipping through her pussy lips fills the air along with the scent of her arousal. A deep groan erupts at the intoxicating combination. How am I supposed to focus on driving safely when she's so close—so slick and ready for me?

It doesn't take long before her body arches against the seatbelt as she comes, and my hands clench the steering wheel, resisting the need to reach for her. Satisfied after her little show, Poppy slides sticky fingers from beneath her panties, and one thought materializes.

I can allow myself this one privilege. Grabbing her hand, I bring it to my mouth and suck her gleaming fingers clean. "I want more. Do it again."

Her eyes widen before bouncing between the road and me, and I wonder if she's going to deny my request. But like a good mate, Poppy's hand returns to its former placement, and a delicious, *torturous* cycle begins. She gets off, feeds me, then starts all over again until we finally arrive at the cabin.

Exhaustion from her orgasms outlines her features, but we're not done yet. And I don't mind tagging in, now that we're safely stationary. Raising the console separating us, I pat the empty space.

Her brows scrunch in confusion. "I didn't know you could do that."

"I've been keeping it down as a barrier, but no longer. Not with the stunt you just pulled. Lay down, baby." I smack the seat again before circling to the passenger side of the truck. Hesitant at first, she slowly complies, laying flat on the seat with one leg bent while the other braces against the floor.

"Fuck, I'm going to enjoy this." I tug at her boots and jeans until her lower body is bare to me. A shiver courses through both of us, but I can't tell if it's from the blast of cool air from the open door or the anticipation of what's next.

"Asa... Someone will see."

"No one will see. We're miles away from any neighbors. It's just you and me, little flower. And I'm about to eat this pussy properly; no more quick bites." Bending forward, her splayed body is at the perfect height for me to easily seize my prize.

Her thighs and dark curls are glossy with arousal, the light sheen drawing me like a bee to honey. *Or a bear...* My tongue spears between her sweet folds—the first time I've ever tasted a woman—*my woman, my mate*.

The first touch to her sensitive clit causes Poppy to jump, and I growl at the immediate response, tracking every movement and reaction for future use. I may be new to this, but I'm going to make damn sure she doesn't know that particular truth until after I've made her come so hard it doesn't matter.

CHAPTER SEVEN

POPPY

My tired limbs quake under the building pressure of another orgasm as Asa's mouth continues to devour me like I'm the last meal he's ever going to eat. And holy hell is it hot being so necessary to him. Not to mention how exquisite it feels to be on the receiving end of such passion.

My hand was starting to cramp from earlier, and despite the hottest sexual encounter of my life, it needed a break. The brazen part of me that began this wild escapade had been ready to concede to practical me who needed a nap.

Which I still want, but after Asa's had his fill. A moan of pleasure bubbles over as his lips encircle my clit and begins a rhythmic sucking motion. The obscene sound emanating from him forces another gush of arousal from my core. God, I love those hungry growls he's making. They're so primal and animalistic. Makes me feel like I'm in one of those paranormal romances with claimings and mates—like I'm the only woman he's ever wanted or will ever need.

One hand tangles in his long hair, searching for purchase, while my sore hand rests limply on the seat as my entire body sinks into the leather, too fatigued to do much more than twitch and moan at the cascading waves of another climax.

A daze settles over me—my physical form becoming weightless as I drift in a sea of contentment.

What is happening?

Never in my life would I have thought I'd be naked outside—never would have believed I'd have a man so eager for me he wouldn't care where we were. Yet, here's Asa with his hungry mouth and pawing hands marking my thighs with his bruising grip.

And I fucking love it.

When he finally tears himself away from my oversensitive core, I lazily lift my lashes to see him swipe an arm across a shining mouth, though his beard still holds drops of my dew. "You're a sweet little flower, aren't you? Gonna need to drink from you every damn day to stay satisfied, and even then I doubt it'll be enough."

I shudder at the implication—of him keeping me, of his mouth never straying far from my needy pussy.

"You think you can handle that, baby?"

Nodding, I struggle to sit up until he grasps my arm and pulls me into his waiting embrace. "I'll be happy to try, if it's what you want."

"I want it all. Your body. Your heart. Everything." My breath catches at the startling declaration. For all of my musings about mates and forever, I didn't truly believe Asa would want those things, too. The shock of hearing he does sends my heart into a galloping rhythm of amazement and nerves.

What if he changes his mind? What if we're not thinking clearly because we're caught up in hormones and the romantic story of him rescuing me this weekend? What happens come Monday?

Questions swirl around my mind, dissipating the pleasant buzz from the previous orgasms.

"But you don't want to give me those parts of you, do you?" He backs off, and his absence leaves me cold. "I see the fear in your eyes. It's too much, and I shouldn't ask it of you. Fuck, I'm an idiot." An angry hand shoves his hair back in a frustrated gesture as he stomps away.

"No, wait..." I scurry out of the truck and wince at the sharp rocks underfoot. Grabbing my haphazardly thrown jeans, I yank them up my legs before racing after Asa, leaving my boots behind. "You've got it wrong; it's not too much."

He paces the length of the porch, ignoring my plea, clearly still beating himself up. And I hate it. His obvious pain and self-derision cuts me deep because it's a predicament I recognize—I'm no stranger to hating on myself.

"I mean it's fast, and I'm worried you'll regret everything you've said after tomorrow, but I want this, too. Don't belittle yourself or call yourself names because you're not an idiot or a beast or—"

Asa swiftly advances, driving me backwards until I slam into the cabin wall. His arms land above my shoulders, caging me between the wooden logs and his huge body. A fierce, guttural sound emerges from him as his lips burrow through my hair to nip my ear.

"I am a beast, little flower. Too ugly and rough for my delicate Poppy, but you don't need to worry about me changing my mind. For as long as you'll have me, I'm yours because you sure as hell have been mine from the moment I pulled up to your car yesterday."

Nipples pebbling and thighs clenching, desperate need overshadows anymore of my concerns, his promise serving as the catalyst. "Enough talking." My body arcs into his for relief from the tension coiling inside. "More action. Logically, I hear you, but I need to feel you—to have the proof."

To know the weight of your body as you fuck me.

"By the end of this weekend, you'll know who you belong to. You'll carry my marks all over this sweet body, a map of love bites warning other men to stay away." Each word punctures the last of my guard as he drags me to the front door, and we stumble inside the cabin. "My seed will fill your cunt, dripping down your thighs, so you never forget who owns you."

Good lord, I shouldn't yearn for such a base act, yet my core aches—empty and waiting. We shuffle towards the staircase leading to the master bedroom, but Asa's too impatient and takes me down to the hardwood floors like a predator intent on his prey.

Yes, take me.

Own me.

I'm yours.

CHAPTER EIGHT

ASA

P*oppy is mine.*
The knowledge beats in time with my heart.
Mine. Forever.

Grinding my hips into hers, I let Poppy feel the full weight of my body anchoring her to the ground—urging her to recognize my dominance and the permanence of our relationship. There's no going back now.

The taste of her cream clings to my tongue, and soon it will coat my dick. No one else will ever know her as intimately. *Or as thoroughly...* Because I plan on tracing every freckle and vein with my tongue until every inch of her skin bears my claim.

"Asa..." She wiggles underneath me, her hands bunching into the fabric at my shoulders while I remain immovable—solid sinew and bone with a steel rod ready to plumb her sweet depths.

"You're overdressed, baby." Deja vu hits as I discard her jeans before wrestling her shirt and bra off her writhing form. Her frenzied need emboldens the roused caveman inside, lush curves jiggling with each movement and calling for my dominance to restrain her for my pleasure.

Poppy licks her lips once she's completely bare and eyes my covered form. "So are you. And as much as I like the lumberjack motif, it's time to go." She attempts to unbutton my flannel, but she's rushing too much to maneuver the tiny buttons.

Quickly, I shift back and rip the offending shirt off, the snap of falling buttons tip-tapping across the floor. But who cares about one ruined shirt when I have my woman begging for us to be skin to skin?

Shimmying out of my boots and jeans, I bring my body back to hers, and we groan at the heated contact. Hard lines meet soft curves as I settle over her.

"Damn, baby. You feel so good, so right. You were meant to be mine, weren't you?" Dropping my head, my teeth bite at the exposed spot where her neck and shoulder meet before sucking hard and leaving behind my first mark of possession. It's archaic—something a barbarian would do—but it won't stop me from adding more to the collection.

I wasn't kidding about staking my claim and cautioning others that dare mess with my mate.

"Yes, only yours," Poppy agrees, her legs wrapping around my waist to hold me closer. The fact that she reciprocates my need, matches my hunger, pushes me over the edge and conscious thought is abandoned as I descend on her like a salivating beast.

Squeezing her lush tits together, my mouth nips and sucks her berry-colored nipples, an intriguing flush darkening the areolas before spreading over her chest. I follow the colored border of raised bumps with the tip of my tongue before flicking each sensitive tip.

"Someday, I'm gonna fuck these with my cock and spill my cum all over your beautiful breasts—smoothing it into your skin—so my scent's imprinted on you."

A mewling cry exhales from her throat as he claws at my scalp, urging me forward. "You like that, don't you, little flower? A secret part of you loves the idea of being completely owned by your man—no matter how depraved I am. Isn't that right?"

Poppy's blue eyes flare in assent, another garbled "Yes" renting the air. And satisfaction pounds in my chest. Positioning my leaking cock between her thighs, I trace the opening with the tip before pressing to her center.

She's fucking tight, and her body stiffens at the invasion. Concern batters away some of my lust at the change, and I ask, "Are you alright? I don't want to hurt you." I'm a big motherfucker, and my cock's no different.

"I'm fine, just adjusting." Poppy's face turns pale, and I stop, afraid of moving forward. "I probably should've mentioned I'm a virgin. Just go slow, and we'll be good."

"Are you sure?"

"Positive." A gentle hand cups my cheek. "I don't want to stop."

Nuzzling her palm, I release a pent up breath and nod. "Okay... If it makes you feel any better, this is my first time, too. Though I know it's not exactly comparable." I'm not the one being breached by a fucking steel pipe.

"No, it helps. Except it's probably because of those mean girls and their bullying, huh? Which just makes me angry and sad."

"We're heading in the wrong direction if that's how you're feeling." Reaching a hand down, my thumb slides across her clit. "Don't think about them. Think about us. This." I continue my ministrations, her body relaxing and allowing my cock to slip deeper—inch by slow inch.

Poppy massages my neck before tilting her head and grazing a tender kiss over my lips. "You're right. We're all that matters." Our tongues meet in a languid dance of affection and passion, serving as a pleasurable distraction until Poppy's heat engulfs my thick cock.

A shudder courses down my spine, and a thin film of sweat rises on my skin. *Fuck.* How am I supposed to maintain any sort of control with her body and scent surrounding me?

Swallowing hard, my hips start a pounding rhythm—no finesse, no more caution. I need her to come before my threadbare restraint frays into oblivion. Licking along the mark I left earlier, I growl as Poppy shivers at the action, a glaze of exhaustion appearing on her face. "Come for me, little flower. I know you're tired; you've been through a lot today. Just give me one more."

Back bowing, her pussy clamps down on my cock in release, and I send up a prayer of thanks as my own orgasm erupts, body shaking in relief. I collapse to Poppy's side, our harsh breathing mingling in the ensuing calm.

True happiness and contentment burgeons in my blood. Something I've never felt before in my life, and it births a fear of what will happen if I ever lose it—lose Poppy.

"Next time, let's make sure you have a rug in this hall." The odd statement makes me laugh until two things dawn on me. She plans on there being a next time, and she must be extremely uncomfortable on these hardwood floors—devoid of any semblance of cushioning.

"I'll order one online later. You can pick it out." Rolling to my feet, I bend to ease Poppy off the floor. "But first, you need a nap."

Cradling her in my arms, I ignore her protests of being too heavy and head towards the master bedroom with my precious cargo. Time to prove I'm worthy of more than a fuck—show how I can care for all of her needs.

CHAPTER NINE

POPPY

Sunlight warms my cheek, and I stretch in the soft glow. Sore muscles remind me of last night, bringing a sleepy smile to my face.

Asa had been wonderful, so tender and kind. After settling me on his bed, he'd run a hot bath and proceeded to wash the remaining effects of our lovemaking away. Despite his comments about having bear paws for hands, his touch had been gentle, hardly Beast-like.

"Mmm... I like waking up next to you, baby. That sweet little sound you just made makes me imagine all sorts of filthy ways to hear it again."

Turning to face him, I cuddle deeper into his chest, enjoying the scratch of his chest hair. "I like it, too, though you generate a lot of heat. We need to open a window or get some fans in here at night, so I can sleep without burning up."

Asa chuckles. "I'll add fans to the list along with the rug, but if you need help sleeping, I know a surefire way to wear you out." His hand sneaks under the covers to capture one of my breasts in a possessive hold.

"Maybe you should remind me... for research purposes," I tease, closing the space between us. And Asa accepts the challenge—proving his theory correct over and over again.

Best Sunday ever.

"YOU'RE SURE IT'S SAFE?" Asa asks the mechanic for the hundredth time, and I appreciate his thoroughness. The man had called this morning with the cost and repair needed, and now it's done. I can drive home as if this weekend never happened. As if I didn't fall in love with Asa over the course of the past forty-eight hours.

"Yep, she's all good to go. Nothing to worry about. We just need payment, and you're free to leave."

Stepping forward, I offer my card before Asa and I walk back outside. We stand quiet and awkward by my car, unsure of our next step. A lot of promises were made this weekend. Promises I believe Asa meant, but in the cold light of Monday—away from his cozy cabin—it's easier for doubts to creep in.

"You'll call me when you get home? To let me know you made it safely?" There's a vulnerable look in his eyes, an expression compelling me to soothe his apprehension.

Twining my arms around his waist, I enfold him in a protective hug. "Yes, the moment I'm parked I'll let you know. And we'll see each other soon. It's not that far of a drive." Before this weekend, I would've balked at putting any kind of pressure on someone to drive to see me, not wanting to inconvenience them. But Asa's shown me how I'm worthy of affection—that I matter, that I'm not too much.

"No, it's not. You'll probably get sick of seeing me so much." His tone tries to lighten the mood, but an underlying insecurity seeps into his voice.

"Never." Bouncing to my tip toes, I place a heartfelt kiss on his mouth, pouring every ounce of love into the embrace even if I can't say the words yet. "See you soon."

Asa releases me begrudgingly, and I get into the car before waving good-bye. This time I take the ramp to the highway, bypassing the country roads. Cars fly by me while a sick knot grows in my stomach as High Ridge and Asa get further away.

This is wrong.

The conviction deepens the longer I drive, and by the time I pull into my apartment's parking lot, a decision crystallizes in my mind. *I don't belong here anymore.* Not in Everton. And certainly not alone in my apartment.

I belong with Asa.

If it weren't for my rational brain trying to exhibit some control, I never would've continued with this ridiculous plan of dating like a normal couple, living separate lives. Not after what we experienced this weekend.

I love Asa but didn't want to tell him because it's too early. Too fast.

Well, too damn bad.

After texting Asa I made it home okay, I race up to my apartment, assessing everything that needs to be done. Breaking my lease won't be fun, but it's necessary. Along with packing my meager belongings, but at least I have someone to rely on now. Someone who will help. *And has a truck.*

The thought makes me grin, and I throw the essentials into my suitcase before lugging it down to my car. Tory's going to think I'm crazy for doing this. Same for all of my friends. *If you even stay in contact.*

Which is a big if considering our tenuous friendships. We barely hung out living in the same city; I'm not sure they're going to want to visit High Ridge to see me. But somehow the realization isn't as painful as it once was.

Because I have Asa now.

Excitement blooms in my chest, and once my car's packed, I begin my journey back to High Ridge.

To Asa.

To my future.

CHAPTER TEN

ASA

Watching Poppy drive away from me was the hardest fucking thing I've ever had to do. Saying good-bye despite knowing it wasn't permanent gutted me like a fish out of water.

I didn't want her to leave but understood her reasoning. At the heart of everything, the harsh truth is we've known each other for two days. A blip in a person's lifetime, yet it shook my world. I fell in love. *Me*—the fucking Beast of High Ridge. But she left, and I have to settle for weekend trips until she's comfortable with more.

Sighing, I burst out of the truck as soon as I'm home, an excess of energy riding me hard. And without my preferred outlet—fucking Poppy—I resort to my next favorite activity for calming down. Tossing my shirt aside, I grab the axe stuck in a block of wood and start chopping away.

Physical labor always provides the release I need, though this time it's proving more difficult to discharge the burn in my blood. Sweat slicks my coarse palms, evidence of time passing, and I bury the axe blade into a stump, chest heaving in exertion.

The unmistakable crunch of tires pulling up the driveway drifts back to me, and I round the cabin to see who's visiting. I already told Rhett and Micah I wouldn't be at the lumberyard today, so it doesn't make sense for them to drop in uninvited.

A familiar grey Camry parks by my truck, and hope slams into my ribs as my heartbeat picks up speed. Poppy climbs out of the driver's seat and walks towards me. "You're back," I state the obvious, incredulity coating the words.

"And staying, if it's okay." Wringing her hands nervously, she continues, "I love you, Asa. Which means I don't want to live any amount of distance away from you. I want to be here with you. For good."

Poppy loves me.

Striding forward, my hands cup her face, a tremor spiraling down my body. "Of course, you can stay here; I never wanted you to leave, baby. You're mine, and I love you. That shit means forever."

The brightest smile transforms her beautiful face, and I can't resist tasting a bit of sunshine for myself. The kiss is meant to be soft and sweet—an affirmation of our love—but it rapidly devolves into a hot maelstrom of fervent need.

"Easy, little flower, or else we'll end up fucking on the gravel. And if you thought the hardwood floors were rough..."

Poppy laughs and covers her mouth in embarrassment. "Sorry, I don't know what comes over me when I'm with you. It's like I morph into a sex-crazed nympho."

"Hey, I'm not complaining. My offer still stands: jump me whenever you want. But make sure you're prepared for the consequences whether they be gravel or hardwood."

"I'll keep that in mind." Her hands skim over my bare chest, and I remember I'm a sweaty mess. But before I have a chance to apologize, Poppy hums in pleasure. "You really do pull off this whole lumberjack thing. Were you chopping wood again?"

"Yeah, I needed to burn some energy after you left."

"Hmm... it agrees with you." She draws her nails lower, scraping over the trail leading to my hardening cock. "I saw you the first morning after I was stranded. Out here looking sexy as all get out."

"I know. I saw you, too."

Surprise causes her to look up from her focus on my naked chest. "You did? But you acted so normal."

"Because if I dragged you to the ground for a brutal fucking like I wanted, it might have ended with me behind bars."

"Oh." Arousal sparks in her eyes; the threat obviously not as repellant as I originally thought.

Clutching Poppy's hand, I hurry us back to the cabin. "And that's my cue to take this inside. You're so easy to read, baby. Every emotion is clear on your pretty face."

"That's not very comforting to hear. A woman should be able to keep her secrets."

"Not from her man," I argue, slamming the front door and climbing the stairs to my bedroom.

She mumbles a sound of disagreement but doesn't force the issue. After all, we have more important things to attend to. *Like loving my mate all night long.*

Guiding Poppy to the mattress, I rub the area over my heart at the sight. Against all odds, I landed the girl—the perfect woman for me.

A lush beauty for the Beast.

EPILOGUE ONE

POPPY

ONE YEAR LATER

"**A** re you listening?" Asa grouses from his crouch by the car.

"Why? Is there going to be a quiz at the end?"

"There might... And if you fail, you're getting spanked."

"Hmm, doesn't seem like much enticement to pay attention then." I smile cheekily, loving the dark smolder forming on his face. He's trying to teach me how to change a flat tire in case of an emergency, but I'm not interested. *Maybe later.* Because all I'm focused on right now is how good my husband looks in flannel and jeans.

Wiping dirty hands on a rag, he shakes his head in mock disapproval. "You enjoy getting in trouble too much. How am I supposed to teach a lesson when you're set on being ornery? Damned if I do and damned if I don't."

Bracing my hands on the counter lining the garage, I hop onto the wooden top, spreading my legs in invitation. "I'd prefer you do... me, preferably."

He laughs at the corny line, but the heat in his eyes lets me know he's fully on board. My dress tumbles down my legs and cool air brushes across my bare center—not the most practical outfit to change a tire in, but that was never my initial goal.

"You really are trouble walking around with your pussy exposed and waiting for me. Was this your plan all along?"

"Maybe... I promise I'll learn eventually, but it's not like I don't have you to come to my rescue. Again. Or even Rhett or Micah, if needed." That's one of the biggest changes in my life since moving to High Ridge to be with Asa. I have people now—a support system. Between my husband and his friends and their partners, I don't feel so alone anymore or like an outcast.

Asa drags a chair over and sits before me, his hands sliding up my legs. Bending forward, his lips trail over the fragile skin of my thighs. "True," he murmurs. "You'll always have me."

"Because you love me, right?" I love hearing him say the words, thirsty for them after so long of a drought before meeting Asa. Like I predicted, my previous friendships fell by the wayside. However, instead of chalking it up to a problem with me—something I would've done prior to Asa—I knew it was just the cycle of life and friendships. It wasn't personal.

"I fucking adore you, little flower. At times, I can't breathe with how much I love you." He kisses my clit in affection, his tender gaze meeting mine, and unexpected tears well up at how lucky I am.

This miracle of a man is mine.

All because my car decided to clunk out on the side of the road, delivering my very own prince charming disguised as a Beast.

EPILOGUE TWO

My heart pounds as I track my prize behind a giant boulder. Placing a steadying hand on the cold rock, she pauses, clearly straining to gauge my location above the sound of branches cracking and animals running through the forest.

"Gotcha! Now, you're mine." Poppy yelps in surprise as my arm snakes around her waist, whipping her back into my firm chest. We enjoy playing chase in the woods—playing up my former *Beast* moniker—and it never fails to get our blood pumping in arousal.

"I'm always yours," she admits, breathless after our play.

I tilt her head with a gentle hand that spans her neck in a possessive grip. "And you always will be," I growl before my lips take what's mine. It's time to enjoy the spoils of the hunt: Poppy, my wife.

A rumble of pleasure vibrates in my throat at her familiar taste, and the pain from her nails digging into my forearm heightens my senses. Five years together—four of those spent as husband and wife—and I never tire of my little flower. Sweet and delicate like her name, yet strong and resilient, too.

She survived those years spent alone just like me, and now we have our daughter, Chloe, who fills our lives with so much joy. And some of the townspeople have started to soften towards me. Apparently, having a wife and kid counts in my favor for not being as beastly as previously believed.

"You've caught me, so what will you do with me?" Poppy rubs her ass against my front, knowing exactly what happens next.

"Fuck you raw until my seed takes root. I want you full and round again with our baby." She moans and increases the pressure on my cock in anticipation. We've talked about having another child for awhile, so I know it's something she craves.

Poppy is a wonderful mother—attentive and understanding. And I'm determined to give my wife everything she desires. Her joy brings about my own; it's something I'll never take for granted.

Life gave me my soulmate all those years ago.

And I'll never stop trying to deserve the gift of Poppy—my little flower.

Don't miss Micah's story in Claimed by the Woodsman!

Micah's the younger, easygoing face of the lumber company he runs with his friend, Asa, and older brother, Rhett. With charm to spare, he's never had trouble landing a woman...at least for a short while. But now he's ready to settle down and keep the curvy woman from the bar who's returned to his life with a little extra surprise...

Kate wants a family. After dumping her longtime boyfriend, she decides to cut loose at a friend's bachelorette party where she meets a handsome mountain man stranger. Sparks fly in a dark alley, and what was only supposed to last a night ends up having life-changing consequences...

Can these two lovers reunite to find love while dealing with the repercussions of their sexy tryst?

Short and hot, get ready to start with a bang! A surprise baby is on the way, and this rugged lumberjack isn't about to let it or his woman go without a fight.

THANKS FOR READING & DON'T FORGET TO RATE/ REVIEW!

Please consider leaving a rating/review on Amazon, Goodreads, Instagram, TikTok, and/or any other sites you review on.
Ratings & reviews are the #1 way to support an indie author like me.
They don't have to be long or even positive (though I hope you enjoyed this book!). All the algorithms care about are QUANTITY.
The more reviews, the more my books are shown to other potential readers!
And they serve as guides to readers on whether or not to take a chance on an indie author.
I appreciate your support!
XO, Hallie

ABOUT THE AUTHOR

Hallie prefers steamy, insta-love stories where curvy girls are claimed by filthy-talking heroes. And when she ran out of reading material, she decided to write her own stories. If you want a quick, hot read, she's your girl!